PUFFIN BOOKS

# ATTACK OF THE TENTACLED TERROR

Susan Gates was born in Grimsby. Her father was a guitar player and her mother a tailoress. At secondary school her favourite reading was science fiction – she read every science fiction book in Cleethorpes public library. She also had a craze for all kinds of American literature, especially detective stories, and went on to study American literature at Warwick University. Then she became a teacher and taught in Malawi, Africa (she still has a scar on her ankle from a mosquito bite that went septic), and in County Durham, England. She has three adorable teenage children (she has to say that – they might read this book!): Laura, Alex and Chris.

Previously published as *Sea Hags, Suckers and Cobra Sharks*.

# SUSAN GATES

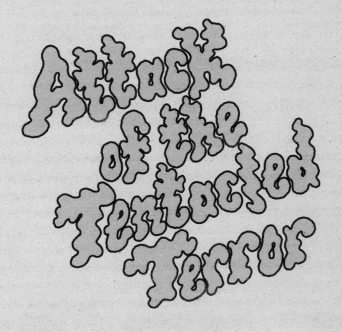

Attack of the Tentacled Terror

PUFFIN BOOKS

## PUFFIN BOOKS

Published by the Penguin Group
Penguin Books Ltd, 80 Strand, London WC2R 0RL, England
Penguin Putnam Inc., 375 Hudson Street, New York, New York 10014, USA
Penguin Books Australia Ltd, 250 Camberwell Road, Camberwell, Victoria 3124, Australia
Penguin Books Canada Ltd, 10 Alcorn Avenue, Toronto, Ontario, Canada M4V 3B2
Penguin Books India (P) Ltd, 11 Community Centre, Panchsheel Park, New Delhi – 110 017, India
Penguin Books (NZ) Ltd, Cnr Rosedale and Airborne Roads, Albany, Auckland, New Zealand
Penguin Books (South Africa) (Pty) Ltd, 24 Sturdee Avenue, Rosebank 2196, South Africa

Penguin Books Ltd, Registered Offices: 80 Strand, London WC2R 0RL England

www.penguin.com

First published as *Sea Hags, Suckers and Cobra Sharks* by Puffin Books 1998
Reissued in Puffin Books 2000
This edition has been produced exclusively for Nestlé Cheerios and
Honey Nut Cheerios 2003
2

Filmset in Monotype Baskerville

Made and printed in England by Clays Ltd, St Ives plc

British Library Cataloguing in Publication Data
A CIP catalogue record for this book is available from the British Library

ISBN 0–141–31667–5

# Chapter One

'This is an emergency!' said Mum, checking her diary. 'The school holidays are only a week away. What are we going to do with George?'

I was busy zapping little green aliens on the computer screen. But I turned down their screams so I could hear what Mum and Dad were saying.

'Well, I can't look after him,' said Dad. 'I've got very important business in Brussels.'

'Well, I can't,' said Mum. 'I've got a conference in Cardiff.'

'Can't you take him with you?'

'Impossible! Why can't you take him with you?'

'Impossible!'

'I could always stay here,' I suggested. 'Like that kid in *Home Alone*.'

'Impossible!' they both shouted.

*Whoosh, whoosh!* I fired my flamethrower and a couple of aliens melted.

Dad put down his *Business News*. 'So what *are* we going to do with George?' he asked Mum.

'I am here, you know. I do *exist*!'

But no one was listening to me.

I twitched my specs further up my nose, then

changed to the evil villain and wiped out a couple of earthlings. *Zap, zap!* Die, you puny earthling scum.

'Everyone's let us down,' said Mum, flicking through her address book. 'Mrs Perkins is getting a new hip. Just when we need her! There's absolutely no one to take George off our hands for the half-term holidays.'

Then Mum's finger stopped halfway down the page.

'What about your Aunt Primrose?' she asked Dad.

'Who? said Dad, looking even more puzzled than usual.

'You know, the one who's lived for years in some ghastly little place by the sea.'

'Is she still alive?' asked Dad.

'Of course she is!' Mum was already picking up the phone.

'Who is Aunt Primrose?' I asked. But nobody bothered to answer.

Mum shoved the phone at Dad. 'You ring her up. She's *your* aunt.'

Dad backed away. 'She's my *great*-aunt, actually, though I usually just call her Aunt. But is this a good idea? I haven't seen her for ages. We never had much to do with that side of the family. We thought they were – well, very strange.'

'All right, *you* suggest someone to look after George!' said Mum in her dangerous voice.

Dad took the phone. 'Seems a bit of a cheek,' he muttered feebly, 'to ring her up after all this time.'

'Never mind that,' said Mum. 'This is a crisis situation. Besides, she stayed here once. You remember, for one night, years ago. When she came on a shopping trip to London. So she owes us a favour, doesn't she?'

'I'd forgotten that,' said Dad. And, with Mum's address book in one hand, he began punching in the numbers.

I swivelled round in my chair.

I started to say, 'But I don't know any Great-Aunt Primrose—'

'Shhh, shhh,' said Mum, waving me to be quiet. She wanted to hear what Dad was saying.

'Great!' Dad was saying. 'That's really good of you. That's saved our lives. Yes, yes, yes, yes. See you Sunday.'

Dad put down the phone. He was smiling. 'She'll take him,' he said. 'We can drop him off there on Sunday. Crisis over. I don't know what all the fuss was about.'

He picked up his paper again.

A sort of doubtful expression was mixing with the relief on Mum's face.

'What did she sound like over the phone?' she asked Dad. 'I mean, she must be nearly seventy. Did she sound senile or anything? I don't want to leave Georgie with just *anyone*.'

'She sounded sharp as a razor,' said Dad. 'Once she'd worked out who I was. She even remembers George. Now, what did she say about him? She said, "George is a special child."'

'LOOK!' I shouted. 'I DON'T KNOW ANY

3

GREAT-AUNT PRIMROSE!'

'Yes, you do, George,' said Mum. Her voice was all brisk and businesslike, as if she was warning me not to make a fuss. 'She stayed here once. Drab little person. Very ordinary. Plump, tweedy suit, white flyaway hair. You remember—'

'Of course he doesn't remember,' said Dad. 'He was only four at the time.'

He looked over his paper at me. 'Can't be helped, George, I'm afraid. It'll be a bit dull with old Auntie. But it's only a week. You can handle that, can't you? You're a cool customer. A grown-up sort of chap. And I'll bring you a big, big present back. What about that, eh?'

'It'd better be a very big one,' I told him.

I swivelled back to my game. There were earthlings scuttling all over the place. *Zap, zap, zap!* I got every last one of them.

'I'm so pleased that's fixed up,' said Mum. She scribbled a note in her diary, then snapped it shut.

'Problem solved,' she said.

# Chapter Two

That very same day, I started remembering things about Great-Aunt Primrose. Things that had been locked up in my mind since I was four years old. At first, they were just scraps of things. Like eyes that were wise and kind. And hair that looked like white candyfloss.

Then more and more memories came crowding out.

'When she came to London for a shopping trip, did this Primrose person take any notice of me?' I asked Mum.

Mum shrugged. 'Well, she *did* stay ages in your bedroom. She seemed to prefer your company to ours.'

'She did notice me!' I suddenly remembered. 'She cuddled me in her arms. We talked for ages and ages. And her arms felt all soft and cushiony.'

Then I remembered something else. Something that had happened late at night, that time she came to stay. I was supposed to be asleep. But I wanted to talk to her again. So I climbed out of bed and went looking for her.

Aunt Primrose was standing in front of her

5

bedroom mirror. Her tweedy suit was folded up on a chair. And she was trying on a new swimming costume.

I remember thinking, 'Wow! Where did she buy that? That's the brightest swimming costume in the whole of London.'

It was brighter than a carnival costume. It was the most razzling-dazzling costume ever. It was golden like sunshine – with lime green stripes!

Aunt Primrose twirled and twirled in front of the mirror, admiring her new swimming costume.

Then an amazing thing happened. I couldn't believe it. I crouched in the shadows, goggle-eyed.

Because the pattern on the swimming costume started to spread – all over Aunt Primrose.

It crept up her chest and throat. Then all over her face. Then the golden and green stripes spilled along her arms. They trickled down her pink legs to her bare pink toes. Even her white hair changed colour, like a green and gold fire.

Until the whole of Aunt Primrose was dancing with green and gold tiger stripes chasing each other like waves all over her body!

Then Mum called up the stairs. 'George, are you out of bed?'

And the pattern began shrinking back.

I remember thinking, 'Oh, that's really sad.' I wasn't scared or anything. I wanted to see some more. It was great. Like watching my own private firework display.

But when Mum shouted, 'I'm coming up there!' the fireworks stopped. The green and gold shrivelled back to the swimsuit where it belonged. And Aunt Primrose's legs and arms went back to normal. All pink and dimply, like before.

She knew I was hiding there. I'm sure she did. She seemed to know, by radar or something. Because she winked at me in the mirror. As if she'd put on that show just for me. As if it was a secret between us.

'Come on,' I told myself. 'That couldn't have happened. You were only a little kid then. You probably dreamed it or something.'

'This Primrose person,' I checked with Mum. 'That time she came, when I was four years old, did you say she was *ordinary*?'

'Oh, quite ordinary,' said Mum, stuffing some papers into her briefcase. 'You wouldn't notice her in a crowd.'

'There you are,' I reassured myself. 'Quite ordinary. So you can't really have seen her changing colour. You must have imagined it.'

Then, the next day, I remembered something else.

'She asked me a riddle,' I told Mrs Perkins who came to look after me after school.

'Who did?'

'My Aunt Primrose. When she came to stay with us when I was four. She asked me a riddle. She said, "*The more you take, the more you leave behind.* What's the answer to that, George?" But she never told me the answer. Do you know the answer, Mrs Perkins?'

'I do not,' said Mrs Perkins. 'I haven't got time

for riddles and mysteries. Do you want beans on toast for your tea?'

I thought, 'I'll ask Aunt Primrose when I see her. I'll ask her what the answer is.'

And, big surprise, I was actually looking forward to seeing her! I even felt quite excited about it. There were loads of questions I wanted to ask her. Like: did you really change colour? Like: what's the answer to that riddle? Like: why did you tell Dad that I was special?

# Chapter Three

'I'm going to miss my plane,' said Dad through clenched teeth, 'if we don't find her house right NOW.'

'A mile past the fishing village. Then look out for a track to the left and some twisted chimney-pots. That's what she said, isn't it? She says the locals call it Two Sisters Cove but there's no signpost. Typical! I think we're lost!'

But then I saw them over the trees. Four chimney-pots, twisted like candy sticks.

'Just like Aunt Primrose said,' I thought.

'We're not lost, we're there,' I said, from the back seat. 'Turn left, Mum.'

Mum spun the wheel and we went bouncing down a steep, grassy track.

'There's the sea. And look, there's a house!'

It was clinging to the rocky coast – a sweet little gingerbread house with shutters and twirly chimneys. But right behind it rose a great, grim sea-wall that looked like the wall of a fortress.

There was a padlocked gate across the track. Mum stopped the car. But she kept the engine running.

'Make this quick,' she said to Dad. 'Just hand George over and get away. We'll thank her properly when we get back.'

'We'll bring her a present,' said Dad.

I climbed out of the car and looked at the sparkling waves.

I took a great big lungful of salty sea air.

'I'm going to like it here,' I thought.

Dad strode round, pulled my bag out of the boot and dumped it on the track.

Mum revved the car. 'Hurry up. Look, there she is.'

'Hi!' Dad raised his arm.

There was a person standing in the door of the house. The person waved.

'She looks just the same!' muttered Mum. 'For heaven's sake, she's even wearing the same tweedy suit. And her hair is still a nightmare!'

Dad clambered over the gate. He had his best suit on. 'Drat!' he said. 'I've got mud on my trousers!' Then he hurried up the track towards Aunt Primrose.

I said, 'Wait for me!' I grabbed my bag and slung it over the gate.

I was just about to climb after it when Mum said: 'Aren't you going to say goodbye to your poor Mumsikins?'

So I went back to the car. ''Bye.'

She leaned out and ruffled my hair. I hate that. And she said, ''Bye, Georgie. Be good. Miss you. Phone you tomorrow.'

Dad was still up at the house, talking to Aunt Primrose.

Mum checked her watch. 'What is he doing?' she fumed. 'He knows we're running late!'

*Parp, parp.* She gave him two blasts on the car horn. Seagulls flew up from the rocks, squawking like mad.

Dad came walking back down the track and climbed the gate.

He looked really strange, as if he was in a trance. He was rubbing his right arm.

'Can you see her?' he asked Mum, in a groggy voice. 'Can you see Aunt Primrose?'

Mum shook her head impatiently. 'Not really. She's too far away. But she looks just the same as always.'

'She's got pink rubber gloves on,' Dad said.

'Pardon?' said Mum.

'She was wearing big pink rubber gloves, all floppy, like cows' udders. And she said, "Excuse my gloves. I've just been washing my best china, for afternoon tea."'

'Fascinating,' said Mum, revving the car a bit more. 'But you've got a plane to catch.'

Dad still looked dazed. He didn't seem to care any more about catching the plane.

'No, no, but listen,' he said. 'She took off one of her udders. I mean, her rubber gloves. You know, to take the piece of paper with our telephone numbers on it, in case George needs to phone us. She took the glove off and as she was taking the piece of paper her fingertips brushed mine and I felt, I felt–'

Mum began to wind up the window.

'I felt an electric shock,' Dad blurted out. 'A

11

definite electric shock went right up my arm. In fact, it's still tingling!'

Mum didn't say anything for a minute. Then she said, 'I think, after this business trip, that you should take a holiday. I think you've been working too hard.'

Dad climbed into the car.

''Bye, old chap,' he said through the open window. 'Have a whale of a time.'

As the car backed away I could hear them arguing.

'We must remember to phone George tomorrow.'

'Well, I can't phone him. I've got wall-to-wall meetings.'

'Do you think I haven't?'

'Well, someone's got to phone him—'

Then their voices faded away.

I watched the car until I couldn't see it any more. Then I watched the flash of its windows on the main road. Then that disappeared too. They were gone.

And I felt, just for a minute, really sad and alone.

I sniffed a big juicy sniff. Then I hitched my specs up my nose and climbed over the gate and picked up my bag. I started walking towards the house where Aunt Primrose was waiting.

Now I could take a good look at Two Sisters Cove. There were no nice sandy beaches. Just rocks, leading down to the sea. There was a door in the sea-wall, so you could explore the rocks. You could go rock-pooling, if you wanted to. But I thought, '*Hmmm*, think I'll give that a miss.' Those rocks looked dangerous to me – all slippery and black.

There was one pool in the rocks that was bigger than all the rest. It wasn't a nice seaweedy shrimping pool. It was square and black and deep, big enough to swim in. And there were steps, cut from the rock, going down into it.

'What are those hooks for?' I asked myself.

I'd just noticed them. A ring of hooks like iron claws. They were hammered into a flat bit of rock, next to the pool.

And I was just beginning to think, 'This place is very creepy,' when Aunt Primrose called to me from the house.

'*Cooeee!* George! George dear!'

Her voice was sweet as honey. As soft as doves cooing.

'Coming, Aunt Primrose!' I shouted.

I hurried up the track. My brain was buzzing with all the questions I wanted to ask her. And the most important one of all was: 'What makes me so special?'

# Chapter Four

'What if Aunt Primrose isn't like I remember?' I began to worry, as I was lugging my bag to the house. 'What if she seems like a stranger?'

But as soon as I saw her up close I thought, 'She's just the same!'

Everything about her checked out. Well, almost everything.

She was quite fat, for a start. Even more like a puffed-up cushion than I remembered. And she had the same frizzy white hair. The make-up was a bit of a shock though – that poppy-red mouth and flour-white face. I thought, 'I don't remember that!' Or the purple Doc Martens boots she had on her feet.

'George, is that really you?' she cried, rushing up to me. 'My, my, how you've grown! The last time I saw you, you were hardly more than a baby.'

And she squeezed me so hard with her pink rubber gloves that she made me wince.

But it was the best proof. The best proof of all that she was the same Aunt Primrose I remembered. She was making a big fuss of me.

Treating me like I was special. Just like she had when I was four years old.

I felt like melted chocolate inside. I couldn't stop grinning a big sloppy grin, even though I was miles too old to be hugged.

'Hello, Aunt Primrose,' I said. 'It's really nice to see you again.'

I'd forgotten what her voice sounded like. It was like a lovely warm bath. So relaxing that all the questions I wanted to ask her drifted right out of my head.

'How about afternoon tea?' said Aunt Primrose. 'Would you like that, George? I know you boys have appetites like gulper fish! It's nothing special, I'm afraid. Just crabsticks and kipper paste sandwiches. Do you like crabsticks?'

'Oh yeah,' I said, nodding my head off. 'I love 'em. They're my favourite. I eat them all the time.'

I thought, in a vague sort of way, 'Why did I say that? I've never even tasted a crabstick. I've never even *seen* one.'

But Aunt Primrose said, 'We shall get on, George. We have lots in common. I might look like an old lady. But I'm not what I seem.'

Her shining eyes looked deep, deep into mine and it was really queer because I felt myself getting woozy. I had to hold on to her so I didn't fall over.

'I've got some urgent things to ask you,' I told her. 'As soon as I remember what they are.'

'Never mind,' she said. 'We've got oceans and oceans of time. Let's snatch a few crabsticks, shall we?'

She patted down her frizzy hair. 'These sea breezes play havoc with your hairstyle,' she said. 'I must look a fright.'

'Oh, no you don't,' I told her. 'You look – beautiful.'

'Do I? Do I, George?' she said. She clasped her pink rubber hands together. She was really delighted.

'You and me, George,' she said, 'are going to be friends. We'll be close as barnacles on a ship's bottom.'

And I could feel myself grinning that big sloppy grin. I just couldn't help it.

As we went inside she let something fly out of her hand. It was a piece of white paper.

'Silly me,' she said.

I jumped up to catch it but it got away. A seagull snatched it, then let it go. It twirled into the sea and was sucked under the waves.

'Never mind,' said Aunt Primrose. 'It was nothing important. Only your parents' telephone numbers. Where you could phone if you needed them. But you won't need them, will you, George?'

She gazed into my eyes for a long, long time.

'No,' I said in a dreamy voice. 'Course I won't.'

There was sand in the hallway. Shells and dried seaweed went *crunch, crunch* under my shoes. From one of the dark rooms we passed came a green eerie glow. I saw it, but I didn't think it was odd. Normally I'm always asking questions. They're like fleas, jumping round in my head. Mrs Perkins says 'How?' and 'Why?' are my favourite words. But I

didn't ask any questions just then. I felt weird –
sleepy and calm and not curious at all. As if
something had shut down my brain.

The kitchen had curtains made out of orange
fishing-nets. But that seemed quite normal.

The radio was playing music. As Aunt Primrose
clumped past in her purple boots it crackled like
mad. She switched it off.

'What rubbish music is nowadays,' she said.
'There's no tune to it. I like a good sea-shanty
myself. "Sixteen men on a dead man's chest. Yo-
ho-ho and a bottle of rum." Now there's a good
tune. They don't write 'em like that any more.'

And she turned and stared at me with those
hypnotizing eyes.

'I like a good sea-shanty myself,' I repeated,
dozily. 'They're great. All us kids love them. We
play them on our stereos all the time.'

Afternoon tea was normal.

Aunt Primrose took off her rubber gloves. She
put on a frilly apron and brought out china cups
and silver teaspoons and napkins and plates.

'I like things to be dainty and ladylike,' she said.

'So do I,' I agreed.

Then, *splat*, she suckered her hand to a plate.

She carried the plate across the room and
released it on to the table, with a sound like Velcro
ripping. I didn't even blink.

'Thank you, Aunt Primrose,' I said.

She sat down and shook out her napkin and
spread it across her knees.

17

'Do help yourself to a kipper paste sandwich,' she said. 'I'm going to have one.'

She pointed to a plateful of dainty triangle sandwiches, without crusts.

Then she leaned forward. Her eyes glittered. They locked on to a kipper paste sandwich. She seemed really excited. She got up out of her chair.

I was just going to reach for a sandwich when – *whoosh*, she pounced on them! One arm stretched out and snatched a sandwich and stuffed it into her mouth. *Gulp*, she swallowed it whole.

There was a blur of snatching arms and *gulp, gulp, gulp*, she'd snaffled the entire lot. The plate was empty.

She sat down. She gave a big belch. Then she dabbed at her poppy lips with a napkin, as if nothing had happened.

'Gosh,' I said.

Aunt Primrose swivelled her eyes in my direction.

'Tea?' she said. 'One lump or two? It's just ordinary tea I'm afraid. No Earl Grey or Orange Pekoe. I'm just an ordinary kind of girl.'

'Oh, no you're not,' I blurted out. 'My mum says you are. But you're not ordinary at all.'

Things happened very quickly. First her voice changed. It wasn't sweet any more. It was deep and booming. It roared like an angry sea.

'Not ordinary?' she boomed. 'Not ordinary? Who DARES say I'm not ordinary?'

She seemed to be swelling. Getting bigger and bigger – I cringed in my seat. *Brring, brring*. Alarm bells were ringing in my sleepy brain. But I couldn't do anything about it. I couldn't move a muscle.

The kitchen was going crazy. The green light on the freezer was flashing on and off. The timer on the microwave went berserk. Aunt Primrose's hair exploded like a giant dandelion clock. Some of it shot clean off her head and floated round the room!

Then very, very slowly, she shrank again. She sat down. She stuck her hair back over the bald bits on her head.

'Silly me,' she said, staring deep into my eyes. 'I almost spoiled our lovely afternoon tea. Just as we were getting on so well. Have a crabstick.'

'Thank you, Aunt Primrose,' I said.

While I was munching away on my crabstick there was a strange fluttering feeling inside me. As if something scary had just happened. But I couldn't remember what it was.

I looked around the kitchen for clues. It was hard to see in the dark. When had it got dark?

Aunt Primrose was nibbling a crabstick. She had one suckered to the end of each finger and a teacup suckered to her thumb. I could see her grey wrinkly scalp through her scrappy hair.

But that was absolutely normal.

It seemed the ideal time to ask those questions – the ones that had seemed so important before. I searched around in my brain for them. But there seemed to be nothing in there. Just a lot of clouds. Then I remembered something – something about a riddle. But I couldn't remember what the riddle was.

It didn't seem to matter anyway. I felt so, so sleepy.

'I think,' I told Aunt Primrose, 'I'll have an early night tonight. Is it night yet?'

'Oh yes,' she said. 'It's been night for a long time now.'

As she showed me up to my bedroom we passed that room again. The door was half-open and I saw steps leading down into the green gloom. What was that noise?

'Is that the sea down there?' I asked Aunt Primrose. 'Can I hear the waves? And what's that funny smell? It smells like the wet fish counter in the supermarket.'

But she turned round and stared into my eyes. And any more questions were sucked right out of my head.

'You can't go in there,' she said, kicking the door shut with her purple boot. 'It's really untidy. I haven't done the dusting.'

So I just stumbled behind her up the stairs.

When she'd gone and I was on my own in my bedroom my brain didn't feel so fuzzy.

I thought, 'This place is weird!' Only I didn't exactly know why and it didn't worry me very much, so I stared out of the window instead.

I was really surprised. Two Sisters Cove was silvery with moonlight. It was beautiful – like an enchanted place.

I thought, 'I'll go fishing in the pool tomorrow. I could tie some lines on those iron hooks.'

I was glad that I'd come to see Aunt Primrose. It

felt as if I belonged here. It felt as if I'd been here for ever.

I looked out of the other window. It faced inland, over fields of sheep.

Something moved in the moonlit fields.

What was it? I twitched my specs further up my nose and looked a bit closer. What on earth was it?

Something was creeping about among the sheep. A dark, crouching figure. I watched it sliding along by the wire fence. Then lost it in some shadows. Found it again. It was picking something wispy off the wire – it couldn't be Aunt Primrose, could it?

Just as my brain was getting curious there was a terrific rumbling roar.

I dashed back to the other window.

The tide had turned. Two Sisters Cove wasn't peaceful any more. The sea was like a wild tiger. A massive Hoover seemed to be sucking it up. But it was fighting every inch of the way, clawing at the rocks with foamy fingers, being dragged off, flinging itself back again.

*Boom! Boom! Kerrash!* The noise was dreadful. Like being inside a giant cement-mixer. I slapped my hands over my ears and wished that it would stop.

# Chapter Five

Next morning when I woke up there was sunshine coming through my fishnet curtains.

I jumped out of bed.

I said to myself, 'It's going to be a great day!' But then doubts, like big black crows, started flapping about in my brain.

I thought, uneasily, I ought to be worried about something. I ought to be very, very worried. But that sun looked so bright and cheery ...

'You probably didn't sleep very well last night,' I told myself. 'Away from home, in a strange bed. You probably had bad dreams or something! But it's daylight now. There's nothing to be scared of in daylight!'

I put my specs on. And the world stopped being a hazy place. I could see everything clearly.

I thought, 'Bet Mum and Dad will phone today.'

I listened. But the house was very quiet. Maybe Aunt Primrose was still asleep.

I checked my watch. It was blank. The battery seemed to have run out.

I wrapped my orange fishnet duvet around me and shuffled over to the window. Every time I moved, fish scales fell out of my duvet on to the floor like silver confetti.

I peeped out of the window at Two Sisters Cove. The sky was striped pale pink and grey. It must be very early. No wonder Aunt Primrose wasn't up yet.

The tide was out and the rocks were dry.

'I'm going to go fishing in that big square pool,' I decided. 'Right after breakfast.'

But someone else had got there before me.

It was Aunt Primrose in her tweedy suit and purple Doc Martens. She was just standing there, by the side of the pool. What had she seen? She was staring at one spot. Her eyes were gleaming. Then, suddenly, she sort of lunged forward and plunged her whole head into the pool.

I couldn't believe it! She was still standing on the rock. Her purple boots were stuck there like anchors. Her big tweedy bottom was stuck up in the air. But her head had disappeared up to her neck. Like an ostrich with its head in the sand. Only her head was under the water.

'No one can do that,' I thought. 'I couldn't do that. She must be made of elastic!'

She seemed to have stretched herself like a periscope. Now her head was swivelling round underwater. What was she looking for?

Seconds went by. One, two, three, four, five, six.

I started getting worried.

'Aunt Primrose!' I yelled out of the window, even though she couldn't hear me.

Minutes went by. She still hadn't come up for air. I couldn't even see any bubbles.

Ages went by. I started chewing at my duvet. But I just got a mouthful of fishbones.

'You'll drown!' I shouted through the window. 'Come up! Come up!'

I felt awful. Like I used to feel when I had asthma attacks, when I was little. I wished I had an inhaler with me. *Gasp, gasp* ... I couldn't breathe. I felt as if I was drowning too.

'Do something,' my brain shrieked at me. 'She's got her head trapped in the seaweed!'

I flung my fishing-net off my shoulders and went racing downstairs in my boxer shorts. I didn't even stop to put on my shoes.

I rushed to the kitchen and out of the back door. The sea-wall stopped me. There was a door in it somewhere. But where?

Frantically I rushed along the wall.

'There! There it is!'

The door had a big iron ring for a handle. I turned it and ran out on to the rocks.

I was skidding on seaweed, slicing my feet on barnacles, but I didn't care.

'Aunt Primrose! Aunt Primrose!'

I looked wildly about but I couldn't see her. There was no one by the pool.

'Aunt Primrose!'

Then I caught my foot in an iron hook and crashed down on to the rocks. And when I landed

24

I was staring right into the pool. It was clear as glass. But floating up towards me were some white wispy strands ...

'Oh no,' I thought. 'It's her hair. She's drowned. She's drowned!'

I just couldn't bear it. She'd said I was special. She'd made a fuss of me. And now she'd drowned.

I plunged my arm into the water and grabbed hold of the hair. But there was no body on the end of it. I put my face close to the water and peered through it. It was trembling down there, with light and shadows.

My breath whooshed out of my body in a great big *phew!* of relief. She wasn't in the pool. There were some fish flickering down there. But no one in a tweedy suit or purple boots.

'Wonder where she is?'

But she hadn't drowned. That was all that mattered.

I just sat for a bit, huddled up on the rocks. Now the panic was over I felt really cold and shaky.

Maybe I'd made a mistake. Maybe she hadn't been under the water as long as I thought. Time didn't seem to have any meaning in Two Sisters Cove.

The sun came creeping over the rocks and warmed me up. My brain seemed to be warming up too. I felt better. And I started remembering things. I remembered the riddle, for a start: *The more you take, the more you leave behind.*

'I must ask Aunt Primrose the answer to that,' I thought.

But I was remembering other things as well. They made me shiver, even in the warm sun. They were scary, sinister things.

Velcro hands? Who had Velcro hands that stuck to plates? Whose hair exploded if you called them not ordinary?

I was just starting to get really worried. Then something, I don't know what, made me look towards the house.

And there was Aunt Primrose at an upstairs window.

Did Aunt Primrose really look like that? That red and white face like a clown? That white woolly hair? She seemed to have masses of woolly hair. Even more of it than usual.

'Wait a minute!' I thought. 'Aunt Primrose looks like a freak! She looks like something out of a horror film!'

My heart started to pound: *boom, boom, boom, boom, boom.*

But then she opened the window and leaned out.

'Cooee, George!' she called in that syrupy voice which seemed to suck all my willpower away. 'Breakfast is ready. What would you like? Kippers? Kedgeree? Or there's always crabsticks.'

Her big eyes glowed like traffic-lights. They looked deep into mine. I couldn't take my eyes away. She didn't blink once. She couldn't. She hadn't got any eyelids.

I'd only just noticed that. But I wasn't a bit surprised. Or worried.

I waved back. 'I'm coming, Aunt Primrose.'

I got up from the rocks and started stumbling towards the house.

I didn't think she was a freak any more. 'She's an ordinary person,' I kept telling myself in a robot voice. 'Just a perfectly ordinary person.'

# Chapter Six

I stumbled back through the door in the sea-wall. Aunt Primrose was washing up at the kitchen sink.

'Have a crabstick,' she said, handing one to me with her pink rubber gloves. 'I've already had my breakfast.'

Then she turned her back to me and plunged her gloves into the soapy bubbles.

*Clack, clack, clack.* I could hear my teeth chattering.

'Why am I standing here?' I thought. 'On these cold stone tiles, in my boxer shorts?'

Then suddenly I remembered. I remembered the shock of that wispy hair floating up through the water.

'I was scared you'd drowned,' I told her. 'I ran out to the pool to rescue you. I didn't even stop to put any clothes on.'

Aunt Primrose turned round. Even though I was half in a trance, I could see a strange change in her. Her eyes, chilly and black as the deepest oceans, seemed to melt to a warmer blue. She looked at me, just for a second, as if she was really moved.

When she spoke, her voice sounded kind. 'Don't worry,' she said. 'I won't drown. Though it was a near thing in the Arctic once, when I got scooped off the bottom by a Russian trawler. But I won't drown in the bathing pool.'

'The bathing pool,' I repeated, dreamily.

'That's right, George. It was cut out of the rock a hundred years ago. To make a safe place for ladies to bathe. Didn't you see the steps and the hooks?'

'Hooks?' I couldn't seem to do anything but repeat what she said. My head seemed to be full of cotton wool.

Aunt Primrose sighed. She said, still kindly, 'A bit slow today, aren't we, my little sea-slug? Never mind, can't be helped. I'll tell you about it later. I'll show you some photos. Some very old photos – of me when I was a girl, beside the bathing pool. But now,' she said, as if she was doing me a really big favour, 'I've decided to let you see something. And we must see it now. Before the tide comes in.'

I followed her through the kitchen, to that mysterious door with the green glow behind it. She pushed the door wide open. 'Careful,' she warned me. 'The steps are slippery.' Then she disappeared.

I didn't want to go down into that green glow.

'Come inside, George,' said a voice, soft as a feather bed. 'There's nothing to be afraid of. Come and meet my precious.'

I didn't seem to have any choice. My feet had a mind of their own. They went down the steps. And I had to go with them.

'Yuk!'

My hand touched something squidgy on the walls. It was a blob of jelly – a closed-up sea anemone.

Green light rippled around me. *Drip, drip, drip.* Water was trickling down the walls. All I could do was stare and stare, with my mouth hanging open. We were in a kind of cellar. But it wasn't a cellar really. It was like being at the bottom of a giant rock pool. The rocky walls were covered with seaweed and blue mussel shells and barnacles.

The light came in through slits, high up in the wall, filled with thick green glass.

Pop! I jumped a mile. But it was only a fat seaweed pod, squishing into slime under my feet.

I twitched my specs further up my nose. I peered into the green gloom.

'Where are you, Aunt Primrose?'

'Here I am.'

She was standing by a large glass fish-tank. There were fish-tanks on stands everywhere. And they all had wire mesh on top. So what was inside them couldn't get out.

'That's a puffer fish,' said Aunt Primrose, pointing through the glass.

A little fish with a mouth like a kiss blew himself up into a big football.

'And here's my jellyfish collection.'

Some jellyfish drifted by like ghosts.

'It's a wonderful world under the sea, George,' said Aunt Primrose, her eyes sparkling with enthusiasm. 'Wouldn't you like to go there? It's an undiscovered world! You'd see such sights, George. Such sights. Sea dragons in the Sargasso Sea. Would you like to see them, George? Flying fish, lantern fish, deep-sea jellyfish, pink and green and gold like lovely water lilies ...'

'Oh yes,' I said dreamily. 'I'd love to see all those.'

'Would you, George? Would you? Then you shall see something now. You shall see one of the great wonders of the ocean.'

She tapped on the glass of the next tank.

'And here,' she whispered, 'is my precious.'

Behind the glass I saw arms, writhing about. I could see a bulging bald head. And two eyes that looked horribly human.

'Isn't he beautiful?' breathed Aunt Primrose.

'Oh, yes,' I said, in my dozy voice. 'He's lovely.'

The octopus blushed a crimson colour. Wavy lines appeared on Aunt Primrose's neck. They were pink and purple. Then the octopus replied with jumping blue polka-dots. They were talking to each other in octopus language. Having a conversation.

I knew what they were doing. And I wasn't a bit surprised. It all seemed – perfectly normal. Like chatting to your mates in the school playground.

'He's a deadly predator,' said Aunt Primrose proudly. 'See his beak? That can bite through steel cables. See those suckers? They can stamp circles out of a killer whale. Like a biscuit cutter through pastry! And he's cunning, my precious. He can fall on his prey like a parachute. Or shoot out ink that makes an octopus shape – so they think he's where

31

he's not. Or hide under sand with just his eyes showing and grab 'em when they swim by. Wonderful!'

'Wonderful,' I agreed in my robot voice.

'I'll give you a tour,' said Aunt Primrose, 'of my little collection. But we haven't much time. This cellar floods with water at high tide. There are tunnels under the floor that lead right out to the sea. It's a very convenient arrangement. It means I never have to clean out the tanks. The sea does it for me. And I don't have to feed them. The sea brings in their dinner.'

Slurp, slurp, I could hear the sea creeping through the underground tunnels. See the water already coming up through cracks and holes in the floor.

Aunt Primrose moved on to another tank.

'Meet George,' she said to whatever was in there.

A massive eel-shape squirmed in the ooze. Aunt Primrose lifted the mesh and scratched its back.

'He's sulking,' she said.

Suddenly she dashed back, lifted the mesh and pulled the puffer fish out of its tank. She threw it in with the eel.

'Dinner-time,' she said softly.

The puffer fish blew itself up in a panic. It looked like a stripy black and yellow beachball.

But the eel didn't move.

Aunt Primrose shrugged. 'Oh well, please yourself,' she said. And she lobbed the puffer fish back into its own tank. It shrivelled like a popped balloon, until it was normal size.

I saw all this. My eyes took in every detail. But I saw it all through a groggy haze. Like when you're very, very tired. Or you've just woken up from having gas at the dentist's.

'Such a pity you can't see my eel in action,' Aunt Primrose was saying. 'He can shock you with 300 volts. Magnificent! The Romans kept them in ponds and fed their runaway slaves to them. Excellent after-dinner entertainment!'

I could feel something sloshing around my feet. I looked down. The cellar floor was flooding with water. Sea anemones were springing open, like a field of orange daisies.

Aunt Primrose was annoyed. 'Tut, tut. We'll have to go and my tour has only just started. There's a cobra shark over there. Very rare. Almost extinct. From the deepest of deep abysses. Don't look at him, George. Never look into his eyes. Cobra sharks hypnotize their prey. They make them feel safe. They make them feel that everything is all right and they've nothing to fear.'

Then she stared deep, deep into my eyes until I felt really sleepy ...

'Then,' she said, 'when you're completely at their mercy, they POUNCE!'

'*Aargh!*' I leapt backwards and crashed into a tank. 'Ow! I've cut my hand on the wire.'

'Sorry,' said Aunt Primrose, sweetly. 'Didn't mean to scare you.'

I sucked the blood off my cut hand. 'Ouch, that stings.'

But the pain had woken something inside my

brain. Those bells were going berserk! Ringing inside my head like a fire-engine.

I looked around as if I was seeing everything for the first time. What was I doing down here? In this spooky, seaweedy cellar?

From a tank in the corner came a scratching sound.

'What's in there?' I pointed at the tank. 'Why is it covered up?'

Questions were beginning to buzz round in my brain.

Aunt Primrose glanced towards the tank. It had a blue plastic sheet over it so you couldn't see inside. 'Oh, that,' she said, in a casual voice. 'That's empty. There's no water in it.'

'But I heard—' I started to say.

'You heard nothing!' said Aunt Primrose as we splashed towards the stairs.

But I was busy thinking my own private thoughts. 'I did,' I decided. 'I'm sure I did.'

At the top of the steps I turned round to wait for her.

What on earth was she doing? Horrified, I saw sea water gushing in. With it came glittery fish. I saw Aunt Primrose snatch one out of the water. She let it flap for a minute, stuck fast to her hand.

She wasn't going to – ? Oh yes, she was. My eyes opened wide in shock as she flipped the fish into her mouth. And crunched it up alive, even the bones.

Then she looked up at me with her traffic-light eyes. She stared and stared. Until eating live fish seemed absolutely normal. No different to munching a bag of crisps at breaktime.

She came up the steps to join me, picking fishbones out of her teeth. The water was rising up to the ceiling. The scratching from the big covered tank went on and on and on. Then she shut the cellar door behind us and I couldn't hear it any more.

# Chapter Seven

'What happy times,' said Aunt Primrose, as she turned a page in the old photograph album. 'Carefree times when I was just an ordinary little girl.'

This time I didn't contradict her. Deep in my jelly brain, I remembered that it wasn't a good idea to contradict Aunt Primrose when she said she was ordinary.

So I said, 'You were ever so pretty.'

'Ahhhh!' She gave a hiss of pleasure. 'I was, wasn't I?'

We were sitting at the kitchen table. It was already afternoon but I couldn't remember where the hours had flown. I thought it was still Monday. But I wasn't even sure about that. Since I'd come to Two Sisters Cove I seemed to be wandering around in a dreamy daze. But I wasn't worried about it.

'And here,' said Aunt Primrose, 'is little me again. With my ma and pa this time. And you can see the tent in this one. Where we used to change into our bathing costumes. Look!' she said in a sharp voice. 'You aren't looking!'

I tried to make myself concentrate on the

picture. It was an old black and white photo. And there was a family in it, sitting on the rocks by the bathing pool. Pa in a straw hat, Ma in a big floppy sunhat. And little Aunt Primrose with her hair like Alice in Wonderland, in a frilly frock and white button-up shoes. And behind them a jolly striped tent like a teepee, tied down to the iron hooks.

'It always seemed to be summer then,' Aunt Primrose was saying. 'And I was everyone's favourite. Pa called me his little princess. Look at my golden hair. Everyone loved me. Ahhh! Long-lost happy days!'

She gave a long, sad sigh. She took off her rubber gloves and stroked the photo. She seemed to have forgotten all about me. She hadn't stared into my eyes for a long, long time ...

My brain started to wake up.

'So that's what the iron hooks are for,' I told myself. 'For putting a tent up.' Somehow I'd thought they had a much more sinister purpose.

The photo wasn't sinister either. It was – just ordinary. It was a sunny day. Everyone was smiling. The bathing pool looked liked a shiny mirror.

Except – except there was *something* odd about the photo. I tried to study it but my mind was still foggy.

Got it! Someone had been snipped out. There was a neat, person-shaped hole right in the middle of the photo. That wasn't ordinary. I frowned and turned the page. The next one had a piece cut out of it too.

I opened my mouth to ask Aunt Primrose a question. 'Why – ?'

*Burrp, burrp!*

'Telephone!' yelled Aunt Primrose as she leapt up, knocking the album on to the floor.

'It might be my mum!' I cried, and I leapt up too.

Suddenly I really wanted to hear Mum's voice coming down the telephone line.

'I'll answer it!' said Aunt Primrose. And she gave me a shove – a really hard shove.

'Owwww!' I yelled. But she'd already gone.

A pain, like electricity, shot through my body when she pushed me. The pain fizzled out and left just a tingling feeling. But something had happened to my brain. The shock had jump-started it. Thoughts were fizzing around in there. Just like they used to do.

I picked up the album. And when I did, a shower of little girls fell out of the back of it. I scooped them up and spread them out on the table. They'd all been cut out of photographs. And they were all the same little girl. They were all Aunt Primrose.

'Two Aunt Primroses?' I thought. It didn't make sense.

I turned the pages of the album and, like doing jigsaws, I fitted the little girls into the holes in the photographs. So now each one had two Aunt Primroses in it. Like seeing double.

'Is it trick photography or what?' I thought.

I twitched my specs up my nose and looked closer. 'A-ha!'

I'd found the answer. I could see that the little girl snipped from the photos wasn't Aunt Primrose at all. At first she looked the same. But now I could see some differences. In this photo the second little girl had different shoes.

I turned the page. In this one her socks were falling down. And in all the photos she wasn't as pretty as Aunt Primrose. She had golden hair. She had a friendly, smiley face. But she didn't look like a fairytale princess in the way Aunt Primrose did.

Those warning bells in my head were as loud as cathedral bells!

I flipped through the album again and took the mystery girl out of the photographs. Something told me that Aunt Primrose wouldn't like to see her there when she got back.

I stuffed the cut-out pieces into the pocket of my jeans.

'This is getting weirder and weirder,' I thought.

I didn't feel safe. I didn't feel safe at all.

But before I could get really worried, Aunt Primrose came back from the telephone.

'Was it my mum?'

'No,' said Aunt Primrose. 'It was a wrong number.'

'But –'

She stared into my eyes like a cobra shark.

'Isn't she weird-looking?' I thought.

For the second time, it hit me how gruesome her white make-up was. It was plastered on, thick as Christmas cake icing. And her hair! It was scraggy and tatty. It exploded like dandelion clocks! It floated in pools!

I thought, 'That's not her own hair. That's fake hair!'

Her eyes glowed white hot. She gave me a triple blast of her cobra-shark stare.

Instantly my head went all woozy. 'Oh no,' I thought. 'Not again.'

So I took my glasses off.

I've got bad eyesight. It's really bad in my left eye. When I take off my specs everything goes fuzzy on that side. So I turned my face to the right. Straight away Aunt Primrose became a white blur. I could see her red mouth moving. But I couldn't see her stare.

And guess what happened? I didn't have a cotton-wool brain any more. It stayed sharp. It stayed on full alert!

'Aunt Primrose,' I said. 'You remember that riddle you told me once – *the more you take, the more you leave behind*? What's the answer to that riddle? I've been meaning to ask you ever since I got here. I mean, you did ask me that riddle, didn't you?'

Aunt Primrose looked blank. Just for a second. Then she lisped in a voice all soft and buttery: 'Oh yes, I did ask you that widdle. I wemember it now. But would you believe it, I can't wemember the answer. The answer to that widdle has gone wight out of my head. It's not important, is it?'

I turned my face sideways. When I couldn't see her, even her voice seemed to lose its power. I smiled, ever so politely, and said, 'No, it's not important. It doesn't matter a bit.'

But inside my head I knew it did matter. The Aunt Primrose who came to London wouldn't have forgotten the answer. She wouldn't have said it wasn't important. I felt quite sure about that.

'What's going on?' I thought, squinting out of my left eye at the red and white smudge across the table.

And suddenly I felt very, very unsafe indeed.

# Chapter Eight

I was on my own in my bedroom. At last I could put my specs back on. All day everything around me had been fuzzy. But it wasn't fuzzy inside my head any more.

I looked out of the window at Two Sisters Cove. The tide was out. The bathing pool glittered in the moonlight. There were crowds of stars in the sky. It was nearly as bright as day.

I listened. The house was very, very still. Aunt Primrose must have gone to bed.

I was really worried about her. I'd decided she was very weird indeed. I'd decided I was scared of her. And why hadn't Mum and Dad phoned? And what day was it? My mind was like a washing-machine with questions tumbling round and round.

And I'd started remembering things. Things that hadn't worried me before but that worried me sick now. Did I really see Aunt Primrose playing at ostriches in the bathing pool? Creeping around in that field of sheep? Having a chat with an octopus? Or was I just going crazy?

But there was a problem even more urgent than

all of these. I was starving. My stomach was going, 'Feed me!' It needed something besides crabsticks. I'd had crabsticks every day for breakfast, lunch and tea. There must be something else in those kitchen cupboards. Some biscuits. Or even some crisps.

'They're probably prawn cocktail flavour,' I muttered to myself.

But it didn't matter. I had to have FOOD!

So I made a plan. I was going to:

1. Creep down to the kitchen and search for FOOD.
2. Creep back to the bedroom and scoff FOOD.
3. Worry about whether or not I was going crazy.

I opened my bedroom door a crack. It went *squeak*!

Oh no, I thought. She'll hear it.

I held my breath. But nothing stirred in the house.

So I tiptoed along the upstairs landing.

Then I heard it – a strange, shushing sound. Like the surf on a distant shore. Like listening to a sea-shell.

It was Aunt Primrose, singing to herself.

I should have crept straight past her open bedroom door. But I couldn't. I had to stop and look inside.

She was sitting in front of a mirror, combing her wispy hair. She had her back to me. She seemed really happy and peaceful, singing a weird little song.

'*Under the sea,*' she was crooning,
'*Georgie and me.*
*Oh, how happy we shall be,*
*Under the sea.*'

I should have tiptoed on. I should have remembered those Velcro hands, the electric shock, the cobra-shark stare. But her voice was like a lullaby. It made me feel really happy and peaceful too. Like a little boy who'd come to ask for one more cuddle.

And I nearly stepped inside the door.

Then something terrible happened.

Aunt Primrose's comb got stuck in her hair.

'Bother,' she said.

She gave it a tug. Then another.

And a big tuft of hair came right out of her head.

She went bananas!

'*Aaaaaargh!*' she cried, in a shriek that rattled the windows.

I cringed back into the shadows.

'This sheep's wool is useless!' she screamed into the mirror. 'It won't stay glued on. It's a total waste of time collecting it!'

And suddenly, she was yanking it all off her head in great big handfuls. Her scalp was grey and baggy like elephant skin.

'I'm sick!' she shrieked. 'Sick and tired of pretending! Sick of being ordinary! Sick of afternoon tea!'

She got up out of her chair.

'I've changed my plans!' she cried. 'I can't stay here a minute longer! I'm going back right now!'

And in one horrific moment, with a noise like a whoopee cushion, she started to collapse.

Like a puffer fish blowing out air, her plump body shrivelled. Her tweedy suit fell to the floor. Her white make-up cracked like the ice on a pond and fell off.

And, after the shrinking, all that was left on the carpet was a horrid, grey wrinkly thing squirming around. It had a massive bulgy head and body and skinny, writhing arms and legs.

But it still had Aunt Primrose's big red lips. It had her mega-intelligent eyes. And two of the tentacles still had her purple boots on the end.

'Ahhhhhh!' The Thing on the carpet gave a great sigh of relief. 'That's better,' it said to itself. 'Like taking a corset off. Only the other way round.'

I wanted to race away like the wind. I wanted to get out of there, fast! But my legs were too wobbly to run.

*Clack, clack, clack.* My teeth started chattering. Surely she could hear them?

The Thing sniffed the air. It waved two tentacles, with suckers on the end.

'What can I smell?' it hissed. 'Is that you, George? Come closer, George.'

Then it started to croon its terrible song.

> '*Under the sea,*
> *Georgie and me.*

*Oh, how happy we shall be,*
*Under the sea.'*

My brain was screaming at me: 'Run, George! Run!'

With a superhuman effort, I made my legs walk. I took one tottering step. Then a slithery tentacle shot out and curled round my ankle.

'Come closer, George,' said the Thing on the carpet. 'I've got something to tell you. I'm going back to the sea. But I've grown fond of you, George, while I've been here. So, guess what? I'm taking you with me!'

The Thing was reeling me in like a fish on a line. I stumbled towards it.

'Don't look in its eyes!' my brain was babbling. 'Don't look in its eyes!'

'Just think, George,' hissed the Thing. 'When you grow up, you will be Lord of the Oceans. Dolphins will be your servants. You can hitch a ride on a humpback whale!'

With another superhuman effort, I managed to twitch off my specs.

'No!' I screamed, in a panic. 'No! I'm not coming with you!'

The tentacle tightened round my ankle. But I wrenched myself free. I staggered down the stairs.

'Hide!' my brain told me. 'Hide! Hide!'

I took a quick look behind me. The Thing wasn't following. I hardly knew where I was going, what I was doing. I half-ran, half-fell down the cellar steps, and crouched in that spooky green glow under the biggest tank, gasping for breath and shaking all over.

I was so scared I didn't notice it at first. But then the roaring in my ears died down and I heard it. *Scratch, scratch, scratch.* I looked up. *Scratch, scratch, scratch.* It was coming from the tank right above my head.

# Chapter Nine

I looked up at the tank. I put my specs back on. I still couldn't see inside it – it was covered with a blue plastic sheet. But the scratching noise had stopped.

I peered round the cellar. It was like being at the bottom of the ocean. Soupy green moonlight was coming through the windows. There were fishy eyes and gleaming fangs everywhere.

But the Thing wasn't coming down the steps. The door at the top stayed closed where I'd slammed it shut behind me. Maybe I was safe here for a bit. Maybe the Thing didn't know where I was hiding.

Suddenly, the legs of the tank started to tremble.

'What's going on?' I thought in a panic.

Above my head the tank was rocking, as if whatever was inside was trying to get out.

I thought about what was in the other tanks – the precious, the electric eel, the cobra shark.

And I scuttled like a crab from underneath, just as the blue plastic sheet slid off, *flop*, in a big heap on the floor.

I had to look into the tank. I just had to.

My hand went flying up to my mouth. 'Oh no!'

The tank was full of water. It had wire-mesh on top of it, weighted down with rocks.

And inside the tank, curled up like a giant pink water-baby, was another Aunt Primrose!

For a few seconds, my brain went blank with shock. I just stared and stared, my mouth hanging open.

She had that green and golden bathing suit on – the one she'd bought in London. Her white hair floated like seaweed round her head. Her eyes were wide open. They were looking straight at me.

'Its *my* Aunt Primrose – it's the *real* Aunt Primrose,' I whispered to myself.

And she was dead. Drowned in a tank of water.

My knees started to crumple. Then something astonishing happened. Bubbles came out of her mouth! They fizzed up and burst on the surface of the tank.

I couldn't believe it. I had to hang on to the tank to stop myself falling. She's alive, I thought.

Her lips started to move. More bubbles came out, a whole crowd of them. She was trying to tell me something. But I couldn't make out the words.

'What?' I pleaded. 'What?'

'Get – me – out,' said the mouth. And Aunt Primrose's pink hand waved upwards, towards the mesh.

I stretched up and pushed off some rocks. They went crashing to the floor.

'*Shhhhh! Shhhh!*' I warned myself, with a scared look at the cellar door. But nothing came slithering down the steps.

I heaved off the last few rocks and dumped them on the floor. They were really heavy. They nearly broke my back! I tried to work as fast as I could. But inside the tank Aunt Primrose didn't seem too upset. She was leaning on one elbow, watching me. She seemed quite interested. She was blowing out clouds of silver bubbles.

I pulled back the wire mesh and Aunt Primrose uncurled from the tank. She stood up, streaming with water.

Then she climbed over the edge. 'Thank goodness you found me, George,' she said. 'It was getting awfully cramped in there.'

She gave me a hug. It was a damp, seaweedy, salty sort of hug. But I felt safe straight away. Really, truly safe this time.

I checked her eyes. They weren't cobra-shark eyes. They were wise and kind. I knew for certain that I'd found the real Aunt Primrose. And that the Thing upstairs was an imposter.

Questions were fighting to get out of my mouth. 'Who's that upstairs pretending to be you?'

'That's my twin sister, Violet,' said Aunt Primrose. 'She disguised herself as me. But she's a Sea Hag, really.'

'Why didn't you drown? How could you breathe in that water?'

'I've got gills, of course,' said Aunt Primrose, in the same matter-of-fact voice. She pushed aside her draggly hair. Behind her ear there were four slits in her neck.

I felt dizzy. My brain just wouldn't take it in. My

knees started to crumple all over again. Aunt Primrose caught me. 'Sit down,' she said. 'You've had lots of awful shocks. You've had a dreadful time! Sit down and I'll explain everything.'

I smiled gratefully at her. I let myself sink down to the cellar floor among the blobby sea anemones.

Aunt Primrose sat down beside me.

'She wants to take me away,' I told her. 'She said she likes me and ...'

'Oh dear,' interrupted Aunt Primrose. 'She didn't say she *likes* you, did she?'

I nodded miserably.

'Don't worry,' said Aunt Primrose. 'I'll protect you. I won't let the Sea Hag take you.'

She slid a comforting arm round my shoulders. I couldn't help checking her hands. There were no suckers on them.

'It's all right,' she said, as if she could read my mind. 'I am the *real* Aunt Primrose.'

'I know,' I told her with a deep, deep sigh of relief.

I felt safe with her. Safe from the Sea Hag.

But I still felt bewildered. I still didn't know what was going on. There were so many weird things, so many extraordinary things happening all around me, that it seemed like the most important question in the world.

'Why am I so special?' I asked the real Aunt Primrose.

# Chapter Ten

'I'll tell you why you're special,' said the real Aunt Primrose, as we sat huddled up on the slimy cellar floor. 'But before I do, there are other things that you must understand. Things about your family. About my twin sister, Violet, the Sea Hag.'

I was going to interrupt to ask about the riddle. 'Tell me the answer, please!' I was going to beg her. But her voice sounded so solemn that it drove the riddle clean out of my head.

'Does my sister know you're down here?' asked Aunt Primrose. 'If she doesn't, we're safe here until the next high tide.'

'I don't know. I ran away! I don't *think* she knows where I am.' I gripped Aunt Primrose's arm. 'But I saw her, Aunt Primrose. I saw her shrink and go all bald and wrinkly. I saw her turn into an octopus!'

'Oh dear,' said Aunt Primrose, pulling me closer to her. 'That must have been a terrible shock.'

'Is she really an octopus?'

'She's a Sea Hag,' said Aunt Primrose proudly, as if there was a world of difference. 'There hasn't been a Sea Hag in our family since sixteen forty-two. We thought they'd died out.'

'But she's got tentacles,' I said, shivering just thinking about it. 'She's got tentacles with suckers on them.'

'Yes, she has. But she can also stun you like an electric eel. Hypnotize you like a cobra shark. Blow herself up into a puffer fish, change colour like an octopus—'

'You can change colour,' I interrupted her. 'I saw you once – that time you came to stay.'

'Did you?' said Aunt Primrose, smiling. 'I thought there was someone watching. Yes, I can do that. But that's nothing – it runs in the family. I've got gills too. Only a few of us have those. But I'm not a Sea Hag. A Sea Hag is a magnificent creature! More powerful than any octopus or shark. She can do things that all of them can do – and more. She can grow new sets of teeth like a shark. She can grow new arms and legs like a starfish. I'm her sister – and even I don't know the true extent of her powers. She *may* even be immortal.'

'But how did she get like that? Was she born a freak?'

'A freak?' Aunt Primrose sounded really shocked. 'Where did you get that idea? She's a Sea Hag. She's the Eighth Wonder of the World. She certainly is not a freak.'

'Sorry,' I apologized. 'I didn't mean to be rude – but was she born a Sea Hag, then?'

'Oh, no,' said Aunt Primrose. 'When we were born, she was quite ordinary. An ordinary beautiful little girl. Violet was the beautiful twin. And I was, well, the plain one.'

'I saw photographs,' I told her excitedly. 'She cut you out of them.'

And I dug in my pocket for the snipped-out Aunt Primroses to show her.

'Oh dear,' sighed Aunt Primrose when she saw them. 'That's very bad news.'

'Why? I don't understand. Does she hate you or something? Is that why she cut you out of the photos?'

'Yes,' said Aunt Primrose. 'I'm afraid it is. But look, I'll start at the beginning. I'll explain about our family. And then you'll understand.'

In the tunnels under the cellar there was the sound of sea water. But it was only a gentle shushing.

'The tide's coming in,' said Aunt Primrose. 'But we're safe here for a little while yet.'

As I had when I was four years old, I curled up in the crook of her arm and waited for the story to begin.

'Our family,' said Aunt Primrose, 'has never been ordinary. In the old days they said it was a curse. But now I think they'd call it genetic. Anyway, you know that things run in families – special things, like being able to waggle your ears or lick your nose with your tongue or crack your knuckles?'

I nodded. 'My friend can waggle his ears. And his dad can do it. And his grandad.'

'Well, special things run in our family too. But they're all sort of *fishy* things. What I mean,' said Aunt Primrose tactfully, 'is that some of us, from time to time, turn out to be a little bit like sea creatures. I mean, only a little bit – just webbed toes like my father had, or changing colour, or having slime glands or a fin or two. Nothing much. But then my twin sister changed into a Sea Hag. And that was a different thing altogether.'

'But why?' I asked her. 'How did it all start?'

'What, you mean our family being like sea creatures? Well,' Aunt Primrose shrugged, 'who knows? Why can some people waggle their ears? It's a mystery really. All I know is, it's been going on for generations. We were always a seafaring family, the sea in our blood and all that. And there was some talk, hundreds of years ago, about one of us taking a seal-woman for a wife. But that's a bit far-fetched, don't you think?'

'*Gulp*,' was the only sound I could make. '*Gulp*.' I couldn't seem to find any words.

'All families have their little quirks,' said Aunt Primrose, calmly. 'And we all thought the fishy genes were getting weaker. I mean, it's been ages since anyone had slime glands. So my sister Violet changing into a Sea Hag was quite a surprise.'

At last, I found some words. 'So when did she start to change?'

'When she was eleven. That's when it always happens. I didn't get gills till then. Violet got gills like me, and a few fins. But she didn't stop. She just went on changing. Poor Violet.'

'Poor Violet?' I repeated. I didn't feel at all sorry for the Sea Hag.

'Yes, it was very sad. You see, she wasn't a bit

pleased. When we were little she was the pretty one. She was a bit vain I suppose, and spoiled. But you couldn't help loving her. Everybody did. Everyone invited her to parties. She had lots of admirers –'

'Do you mean boyfriends?' I asked, amazed. 'Didn't they mind about her being a Sea Hag?'

'They didn't know. Not at first. She disguised it very well. She combed her golden hair over her gills. She wore white gloves all the time.'

'To hide her suckers.'

'That's right. But the older she got, the more she changed. Her golden hair started falling out. Her white skin grew grey and tough, like a whale. It got harder and harder to hide what was happening. And one dreadful day when she was seventeen–' Here Aunt Primrose stopped and shook her head, sorrowfully.

'What happened? Tell me what happened!'

'It was a beautiful summer's day – fifty years ago. And Violet was in the tent by the bathing pool. She was getting changed. And her young fiancé, the boy she was going to marry, went creeping over the rocks to surprise her. He called out, "Cooeee, Violet, my darling!" He peeped into the tent–'

I gasped. 'What did he see?'

'He wouldn't speak about it,' said Aunt Primrose in a hushed voice. 'But it must have been something very nasty indeed – because he never got over the shock. He went into a monastery the very next day. And Violet was broken-hearted.'

'Gosh!' I said.

'And after that, Violet became very bitter and vengeful. She blamed me. She said I was jealous because I wasn't pretty and had no admirers. She said I'd told her fiancé her terrible secret. But I hadn't,' said Aunt Primrose. 'I loved Violet more than anything. I wanted her to be happy.'

A tear sparkled on Aunt Primrose's cheek.

'But she was never happy again,' she said. 'She just wanted to be ordinary. She didn't want any special powers. She stayed in her bedroom and wouldn't see anyone. She stayed there for days and days. Then, one night, at high tide, something came slithering down the stairs. It was Violet. She'd become a full-blown Sea Hag. We watched from the window. She slithered across the rocks, waved a tentacle at us and disappeared into the waves.'

Aunt Primrose sniffed bravely and wiped her tears away.

'And I never saw her again until the day your father phoned me. When she turned up for afternoon tea. I thought she'd changed. I thought she'd accepted being a Sea Hag. I even thought she wanted us to be friends. But she didn't. She stunned me with an electric shock. Put me in that tank. She said, "I'm going to be ordinary. I'm going to be like everyone else!" But she can never be ordinary,' said Aunt Primrose. 'No matter how hard she tries. She's a Sea Hag. She's different.'

'She's got fishing-nets all over the place,' I told Aunt Primrose. 'On the windows, on the beds. It looks really weird.'

Aunt Primrose tut-tutted sadly. 'She steals them

from trawlers,' she explained. 'She's got a grudge against deep-sea trawlers. I don't know why.'

Under the cellar floor the shushing noise had turned to sloshing. In the tanks things were moving – scuttling, writhing about, getting excited. They knew the tide was coming in.

'So where's she been all these years?' I asked Aunt Primrose.

She shrugged. 'Who can tell? Roaming the oceans of the world – the Arctic, the Atlantic, the Pacific. Under the polar ice-cap. Down in the deepest abysses. Time means nothing to a Sea Hag. But wherever she's been, she must have been very lonely. As far as I know, she's the only Sea Hag in existence.'

For a minute I felt really sorry for the Sea Hag, under the oceans of the world, all alone. I sighed and shook my head.

Then I remembered she wanted to take me with her.

'How can she take me with her?' I cried to Aunt Primrose. 'I'd drown, wouldn't I?'

'Not necessarily,' said Aunt Primrose, mysteriously.

And she was going to tell me more, when we both heard the noise.

It came from the top of the cellar steps – a sort of shuffling, slithery kind of noise.

It made the hairs tingle on the back of my neck.

'It's her!' I whispered to Aunt Primrose. 'She knows where I am!'

'I thought she might,' said Aunt Primrose. 'She doesn't miss a thing. She's got built-in radar.'

I thought I heard a tiny tremble in her voice.

'Could she beat you in a fight? Is she more powerful than you?' I asked Aunt Primrose, although I'd already guessed the answer.

'She much more powerful,' said Aunt Primrose. 'She's got the powers of a giant squid, a Portuguese man o' war, a cobra shark. And heaven knows what else. But I've only got the powers of a cuttlefish.'

'Oh dear,' I said. 'And she's in a very bad mood as well.'

It made me shiver just *thinking* about her in her bedroom. Wild with rage, ripping her sheep's wool hair out in handfuls.

I twitched my specs up my nose and gazed into the blackness at the top of the cellar steps. 'What's she doing up there?' I whispered to Aunt Primrose.

'Just waiting,' she answered. 'The best sea predators are very patient. They hide themselves. And watch and wait.'

'And then they pounce,' I said helplessly, remembering the cobra shark. 'We might as well give up now. We haven't got a chance. She's going to beat you. And take me away with her to the bottom of the deepest, darkest ocean!'

'Don't talk like that, George,' said Aunt Primrose with a sudden fierce look in her eyes. 'You're special. Always remember that. And we special people are used to rough seas. People think we're drowning. Then we pop up, waving! We're full of surprises!'

I tried to be brave. I gave a weedy little cheer. 'Yay!'

I felt a bit better after that. But I still didn't have enough faith. How can a little old lady with the powers of a cuttlefish defeat a mighty Sea Hag?

But Aunt Primrose was already fighting back. Puffing with the effort, she was lifting up a stone slab in the cellar floor.

'Help me, George. There's a tunnel under here. I didn't want to risk it. But there's no choice now.'

I helped her heave the slab to one side. Underneath was a deep well.

'*Gulp!*' I said when I peered into it. At the bottom you could hear the sea gurgling, like water in a plughole.

'I can't get down there. The tide's coming in. I don't have gills like you.'

'It's our only way out,' said Aunt Primrose. 'Unless you want to go up those steps and face the Sea Hag.'

# Chapter Eleven

'Come on, George,' called Aunt Primrose from somewhere under the cellar floor. 'We haven't much time!'

I peered again into the dark well. I'd taken my specs off and put them in my pocket, for safety. Aunt Primrose's face was just a white moon shape.

'Lower yourself down,' she said. 'And before you go underwater take a big breath and I'll do the rest.'

I groaned out loud. 'I don't want to do this,' I thought. 'I really do NOT want to do this!'

But I was alone now in the cellar. And at the top of the steps the Sea Hag was waiting, with her cobra-shark eyes and horrible snaky arms.

I could hear it! Hear her soft, siren song. It was calling to me.

> *Under the sea,*
> *Georgie and me.*
> *Oh, how happy we shall be ...'*

'Don't listen!' Aunt Primrose shouted from the dark hole.

I slapped my hands over my ears, so I couldn't hear the song any more. I leaned forward to look into the hole. It made me feel sick and dizzy.

'Don't be afraid,' came Aunt Primrose's voice. 'Trust me.'

So I lowered myself into the tunnel.

'Ow!' Sharp barnacles scraped my hands. Seaweed stroked my face.

My feet kicked out. There was no bottom. My hands were slipping on the slimy walls ...

Then, *splosh*, I was up to my neck in the cold sea. It was sucking me down!

But even through my panic I remembered what Aunt Primrose had told me. 'Take a big breath.' So I did. And the water closed over my head.

My eyes were squeezed shut. I was dragged through the water at terrific speed. My ears were roaring, my lungs were burning, there was blackness, icy cold. Someone was gripping my wrists very tight. Then suddenly I was out of the tunnel. Dumped on the rocks outside in a soggy heap, gasping for breath, coughing up loads of salty water.

'Are you all right, George?'

I shook the water out of my hair and forced my stinging eyes to open. Then I felt in my shirt pocket. Good, my specs were safe. With trembling fingers, I put them back on.

And there was Aunt Primrose in the water. Curving through the waves as graceful as a seal. Behind her the sky was in layers like a liquorice allsort – pink, grey, white. Dawn was breaking.

'I'm, I'm all right – I think,' I spluttered.

I felt a bit dizzy though. And the roaring in my ears was taking ages to go away. But I stumbled to my feet. The sea foamed round my shoes. I backed away, up the rocks, and almost fell over an iron hook. I was right beside the bathing pool.

Aunt Primrose came rolling up the rocks on the next wave. She flopped about for a bit, then heaved herself to her feet.

'What happened just now?' I asked her in a dazed voice. 'I went through that tunnel like a rocket. How did I do that?'

Aunt Primrose smiled, modestly. 'That was me,' she said. 'I pulled you along. I wasn't sure I could still do that.'

'Do what?'

'Jet propulsion. It's a cuttlefish talent. You suck water in, then shoot it out at the other end of your body. And, *whoosh*, you're jet-propelled. You can whizz through the sea at amazing speeds. Most exhilarating.'

'Gosh!' I said, my mind boggling. 'You mean, you suck water through your mouth?'

'Yes.'

'And then you shoot it out – at the other end?'

'Yes, yes,' she said impatiently.

'Gosh,' I said again.

But before I could ask any more questions my head suddenly stopped spinning. And I remembered why we were out here, on the rocks. 'The Sea Hag!' I cried.

I grabbed Aunt Primrose's hand. 'Come on, we

have to run away. Run as far as we can. Before she finds out where we are!'

But Aunt Primrose did not move. Her eyes were determined and brave.

'She already knows where we are,' she said. 'I just wanted to get out of that cellar. To fight her on more favourable ground.'

'Fight her?' I gabbled. 'What do you mean, *fight* her? You told me that you've only got the powers of a weedy little cuttlefish. And that she's much more powerful than you.'

'That's right,' Aunt Primrose agreed. 'She is.'

'Then we should run away. Run away now, as fast as we can.'

'We wouldn't get very far,' said Aunt Primrose grimly.

I was petrified. Words came babbling out of my mouth. 'But she'll take me away under the sea and I'll drown and why does she want to take me away ...?'

'She likes you,' said Aunt Primrose. 'And she's lonely – terribly lonely. The loneliness of the Sea Hag is the most terrible loneliness in the world.'

'But I don't want her to like me! Why does she like me? I can't understand it! Why ...?'

But I never got the chance to finish my question. Something yanked my feet out from under me.

'It's her!' cried Aunt Primrose. 'She's in the bathing pool!'

'*Aaaargh!*' I yelled, hanging on for dear life to two iron hooks. 'She's pulling me in!'

A tentacle slithered round my ankle. Its suckers were like a hundred tiny grabbing hands.

'*Ugggh!*' I reached down and tore the tentacle away. *Rippp!* It let go of my leg. But another was already snaking round my other leg.

'Help! She's dragging me in!'

I was stretched out like elastic, clinging on to the hooks. I'd have to let go any second. Only my fingertips were holding on and they were slipping, slipping ...

'LET – HIM – GO!' A voice like thundering surf echoed round Two Sisters Cove. Seagulls flew up, squawking.

And suddenly, *ping*, I was free. I shot back up the rocks. 'Danger! Danger!' my brain screamed at me, and in one quick movement I was up on my feet and ready to run.

But then I noticed the silence.

It was like the strange hush before a storm. The seagulls had settled. The bathing pool looked like glass – not a ripple on it. Even the sea had gone quiet. No Aunt Primrose. No Sea Hag. Where had everybody gone?

Then, *fizz*, a few bubbles came up to the top of the bathing pool.

I crept to the edge and looked in.

And there they were – the Sea Hag and Aunt Primrose. In opposite corners like two prize-fighters in a boxing-ring.

It looked like no contest. A white-haired granny in a bathing suit striped like a humbug. Versus the Sea Hag – a pick 'n' mix selection of the most deadly talents of cobra shark, octopus and electric eel.

The Hag's eyes glowed like searchlights. But this time they weren't pointed at me. They were fixed on Aunt Primrose. Her tentacles writhed about, like they had a life of their own. She'd taken off her Doc Martens. The only bit of her disguise left was her waterproof lipstick. Poppy red lips puffed out from the grey bulgy bag of her head.

I could have saved myself. I could have run away and the Hag wouldn't even have noticed. But I couldn't. Aunt Primrose was in trouble. I couldn't just leave her.

So I crouched down to see what would happen next.

The Hag made the first move. Blast-off!

She shot out an arm like a harpoon. No good. In a blitz of bubbles Aunt Primrose jet-propelled.

'Yay!' I cheered.

But I couldn't see anything. Clouds of sand hid the bottom of the pool.

Then the sand drifted down.

I twitched my specs into place and searched the pool. Where were they? Aunt Primrose was crouched on her chubby legs in one corner. Her eyes were flashing in defiance.

But where was the Sea Hag? There, no there! Among the weed was a purple shadow, Sea-Hag-shaped. Aunt Primrose had seen it too. She edged away from it.

But I had a bird's eye view. I could see what she couldn't. Behind Aunt Primrose, poking up from the sand, was an evil yellow eye. Just one eye, poking up and swivelling.

'A trap! A trap!' I yelled. 'It's an ink trap!'

The purple ink cloud squirted by the Hag dissolved, just sort of fell apart in the water. Aunt Primrose saw it, and knew that she'd been tricked. She froze in her tracks. But it was too late.

Blue light crackled all round her. Her white hair stood on end. Stiff as a kipper, she crashed to the bottom of the pool. The tip of a writhing tentacle began to creep towards her. It was going to wrap itself round her ankle and haul her, ever so slowly, towards that hidden mouth with its seven sets of teeth.

'Aunt Primrose!' I beat at the water desperately. But she couldn't hear.

I started pulling off my shoes, ready to dive in.

Then Aunt Primrose quivered. She flapped like a fish. The tentacles whisked back under the sand. Aunt Primrose came alive.

'Aunt Primrose!' I was nearly crying with joy!

She was still stunned by the Hag's electric shock. She was staggering round in a bubble storm.

Then a grey torpedo shot out of the sand! Shot up to the top of the pool and surfaced right under my nose.

It was the Sea Hag. Aunt Primrose hadn't seen her. But I had. I couldn't miss her. Because she was drifting around on the top of the pool, her tentacles all spread out like party streamers.

Her cobra-shark eyes swivelled round to me. Oh no! But I didn't panic. I whipped off my glasses. But not before I'd seen her wink at me.

'Round three,' she hissed. Then vanished.

I put my specs back on. Just in time to see the Hag floating down through the pool like a grey parachute. I knew what she was doing. She was launching a surprise attack.

Aunt Primrose was still down at the bottom of the pool. She was staring round her, looking for the Hag.

'Look up! Look up!' I yelled at her.

She did look up. Far, far too late. I saw her mouth – a wide, shocked 'O' shape. Then, *blam*, the Hag dropped right on top of her. And she was squashed by that horrible squirmy body.

'Aunt Primrose!'

I saw a flash of green and gold between the Hag's tentacles. A pink hand got free. It waved pathetically.

Then the Hag shuffled about like a monster chicken on an egg. And the hand went limp.

The fight was over. The Sea Hag had won.

I could already hear that spooky song echoing in my head.

> '*Under the sea,*
> *Georgie and me, Georgie and me ...*'

# Chapter Twelve

Special people are full of surprises. Aunt
Primrose had told me that. But I didn't have
any surprises up my sleeve. I just slumped on the
rocks, feeling hopeless, useless.

'Sorry, Aunt Primrose,' I whispered, trying not
to cry.

But somehow, my brain kept on working. It kept
pestering me. Asking me questions: 'How do you
stop a Sea Hag? How? How?'

'What's the use?' I groaned. 'She's just too
powerful.'

But my pesky brain wouldn't give up. 'How?
How? How?'

And a tiny idea started to tickle. Then it became
a big itch.

'I know how!' I thought, scrambling to my
feet.

Slipping and sliding on the rocks, I raced back to
the house. I skidded across the kitchen and ripped
all the Sea Hag's fishnet curtains down. *Ping, ping,
ping* – the curtain hooks shot round the room like
roasting popcorn.

I staggered back through the gate in the wall.

My arms were filled with net. It spread out behind me in orange waves.

I fell on my knees by the bathing pool. My heart was beating like bongo drums. But I gave my specs a twitch, then peered into the water.

'Good old Aunt Primrose!'

She'd fought back. Wriggled out from under the Hag. Those whippy tentacles were already reaching for her –

But I was going to use the Sea Hag's tactics. I was going to launch my own surprise attack.

'Geronimo!'

I shoved the net into the pool, then closed my eyes and hoped it was my lucky day. I hadn't aimed it or weighted it or anything. There just wasn't time.

I opened my eyes. The net spread out on the pool's surface. It wasn't going to sink. Yes, it was. It went billowing down, in netty clouds. But who was it going to trap?

I chewed my lips. I couldn't watch. I had to.

There was scuffling down in the pool – a sandstorm, a terrible struggle. Now the sand was clearing –

'Yay!' I jumped up, punched my fist in the air. 'Gotcha. I've gotcha. Ha-ha-ha!'

Aunt Primrose had jet-propelled out of danger. She was hiding behind some ferny seaweed. And the Hag was trapped under folds of heavy net.

It couldn't have worked out better.

I grinned so hard it almost split my face.

The Sea Hag had gone very quiet.

Why wasn't Aunt Primrose climbing out? Why was she still hiding in the weed?

'It's all right,' I called down. 'She can't hurt you now.'

The Sea Hag's angry yellow eye poked through the mesh.

Aunt Primrose came shooting up, broke the surface of the pool, then scrambled out, dripping.

'Get down! Get down!' she cried. And she flung me on to the rock and shielded me with her body.

Down in the pool the Hag was swelling like a giant puffer fish. As she swelled her eyes got even madder and colours flashed all over her – bright yellow, purple, shocking pink. She was like a living kaleidoscope! The bathing pool crackled with blue electric fire. The water steamed like a thousand boiling kettles. And all the time, under the net, the Hag was swelling, filling up the pool.

Then, suddenly, the net burst into a million pieces. The Hag exploded out of the pool like a rocket launch, trailing tails of fire. I looked up, but I was blinded, like looking straight into the sun. Aunt Primrose pushed my head down to save my eyes.

We crouched down on the rocks. We didn't dare look up. Two Sisters Cove grew quiet again. You could hear tiny waves rustling on the rocks.

Then the Sea Hag spoke.

Her voice echoed round the cove. It was as chilly and dark as the deepest sea caves. Just the sound of it made me quiver.

'Did you think you could trap ME in your puny little net? Me? The Sea Hag?'

Very, very slowly, I raised my head.

'Careful,' Aunt Primrose whispered in my ear. 'Don't look into her eyes.'

Too late. I'd already looked. But what I saw was amazing. The Sea Hag was dangling over a rock like a giant octopus. She still had her rosebud lips. But she'd switched off her cobra-shark stare. And in her eyes there was a new expression. What was it? It was hard to tell. But it seemed to be a sort of mixture – of sadness, pain and pride.

I was still trembling like a jelly. 'I don't want to come with you! I don't want to!'

'Don't be afraid, George,' said the Sea Hag in a scornful voice. 'I *promise* I won't try to take you. I'm not interested in you any more. Not in either of you. Nor in your *ordinary* little lives.'

Her body swelled up. It flushed royal purple. Like Aunt Primrose said, she was a magnificent creature. She was the Princess of the Sea.

Her voice grew louder. It made the rocks ring like gongs.

'I'm going home!' she cried. She flung a tentacle towards the waves. The sea boiled and foamed as if it were answering her.

'Being ordinary isn't worth it,' said the Sea Hag. 'Afternoon tea just isn't my style! I'm the Sea Hag. I'm going home. I'm going back to the abyss! Alone!'

She began slithering over the rocks. The sea made a terrific din like a mighty orchestra, booming and crashing as if it were welcoming her back.

The Sea Hag's mournful cry was even louder than the sea.

'You know where you are at the bottom of the ocean. You can trust a cobra shark. You can trust a cobra shark more than you can trust people!'

I thought she was going. But, suddenly, she turned to me again. She seemed to have completely forgotten her promise!

'This is your last chance, George,' she coaxed in her silkiest voice. 'Won't you come with me?' She swept her tentacle round the bay. 'Do you know how much of this planet is ocean, George? Nearly three-quarters of it! It's so cramped in your little land-world, George. Come to *my* world. Come and explore it. Come and roam the seven seas with me!'

Aunt Primrose gripped my arm. 'Don't listen to her,' she said urgently. 'Don't look into her eyes. Take your specs off!'

But this time, I didn't need to take my specs off. I just shook my head at the Sea Hag. 'I can't come with you,' I told her. 'You know I can't. I'll drown.'

The Sea Hag turned her great eyes on Aunt Primrose.

'So he doesn't know yet?' she said in surprise.

Aunt Primrose gave a tiny shake of the head.

'I'm not coming!' I said again.

'Fool,' hissed the Hag. But she didn't sound angry. She just sounded really sad. 'You don't know what you're missing. But I should have known. I should have known that people always let you down.'

73

She sank beneath the waves. We saw her tentacles coiling like a nest of snakes. Then nothing.

'Violet!' called Aunt Primrose.

But there was only a little crowd of bubbles where the Sea Hag had been. Then, one by one, they popped.

'She's gone,' said Aunt Primrose.

There was a strange stinging feeling in my eyes. And I was really surprised to hear myself murmuring, 'Poor Sea Hag. Poor, lonely Sea Hag.'

'Will she ever come back?' I asked Aunt Primrose.

She put her arm round my shoulders and gave me a hug. We started walking back towards the house.

'No,' Aunt Primrose said. 'I don't think she ever will. I think she's given up on the human race. She's gone back to the fishes.'

'What did she mean,' I asked Aunt Primrose, 'when she sort of stared at you and said, "So he doesn't know yet?" What don't I know?'

'Ahh ...' said Aunt Primrose. She took a deep breath, as if she was going to start a long explanation.

But she didn't get the chance.

For just at that moment, far, far out at sea, a shooting star climbed out of dark blue water.

'It's her!' I cried.

In a burst of glittering light the Sea Hag curved across the sky. Then she plunged back into the sea. She left behind a wonderful golden rainbow.

It was her final farewell.

'Beautiful,' I said. 'She's really beautiful, isn't she?'

'She certainly is,' said Aunt Primrose. 'Beautiful – but deadly, unfortunately. You can't trust her an inch.'

She waved her hand in a last salute. 'Goodbye, Violet,' she called out. 'Goodbye, my dear sister.'

And slowly, very slowly, the rainbow faded away.

# Chapter Thirteen

'I can't believe it,' Mum said, frowning at her diary. 'These school holidays really do creep up on one. It doesn't seem two minutes since your last one.'

I looked up from my book, *The Amazing World of Fish*. It was a present from Aunt Primrose for my eleventh birthday. It had arrived this morning. Right on time.

'So, birthday boy,' said Mum, 'what's it to be this summer? Your dad and I can manage a week at the end of August. Almost certainly. But that leaves,' she flicked over the pages, 'five weeks to fill in.'

She waved a glossy brochure at me. 'Now what about an Activity Holiday? Just look at these children. They look as if they're having lots of fun, don't they?'

I sighed and closed Aunt Primrose's book. I said to Mum, 'Did you know there are ice fish that live in the Antarctic and have anti-freeze in their blood? So they don't freeze solid like ice-pops?'

'Very nice, dear,' she said. But she looked a bit startled. Just like she did when we were going round the supermarket and I filled the trolley with crabsticks.

She said, 'What on earth do you want those for?'

And I said, 'You should try one. They're really tasty!'

I nibbled a crabstick as I looked at the brochure she gave me. There were two children, in yellow climbing helmets, being lowered down a cliff.

'They look scared stiff to me,' I told Mum.

'No, they don't!' she said. 'They're having a lovely time! Now don't be difficult, George; you know the summer holidays are a real headache. Look, I could book you in here for a few weeks. Pony-trekking in Wales! Wouldn't that be great?'

'Or,' I said, 'I could go to Aunt Primrose's. Look at this letter she sent with my present.'

Mum read the letter. As she did her face brightened.

'How convenient. It would certainly solve all our problems. But darling, could you stand it? For the whole summer holidays. Isn't it a teeny-weeny bit boring with Aunt Primrose?'

'I think I can stand it,' I said.

'We'll buy you a present,' said Dad, busy at his computer screen.

'You're already buying me a present,' I reminded him. 'It's my birthday today, remember? We're going to choose some fish this afternoon.'

Mum and Dad threw worried looks at each other. Dad shut down his computer. He swivelled his chair round.

'We've been meaning to ask you about that,

George,' he said. 'Are you sure you want real live fish? In a tank? I mean, they're not exactly hi-tech, are they? Wouldn't you rather have fish on a floppy disc? There are some very exciting biology packages out on CD Rom. The fish look as if they're really alive!'

'I want fish that *are* really alive,' I said.

Dad shrugged. 'Well, it's your present.'

I opened my book again and took a bite from my crabstick.'

'Did you know,' I told Dad, 'that there are fish called mud skippers that walk out of the water and climb trees?'

Mum and Dad tiptoed out of the room. But I could hear them whispering in puzzled voices behind the door.

'I suppose,' whispered Mum, 'it's because he's eleven now. I mean, there are bound to be *changes* at eleven, aren't there?'

Two hours later Dad and I were standing in the fish section of Pet World. I was looking at some goldfish.

Dad was grilling the sales assistant. 'So what exactly do I get for my money if I take your advice and buy this more expensive water pump?'

I stopped listening to them. I was in a world of my own. An orange fish, with a big head like a bulldog, blew bubbles at me, *bloop, bloop, bloop*.

A pink, white and brown one with a frilly tail whisked up to the glass. It stared at me with goggly eyes. It looked really surprised.

'Hello,' I said to it and gave it a wave.

'Oh, no.' I stared at my hand. I couldn't believe it. I twitched my specs up my nose and looked again.

No mistake.

My hand looked like a block of Neapolitan ice-cream! It was striped in layers of strawberry, vanilla, chocolate, just like the fish I was waving at.

The fish in the tank was getting very excited. It darted about in a swirl of bubbles. It bumped the glass as if it was trying to get out.

I closed my eyes and wished, very hard, that my mind was playing tricks. I opened my eyes. The colours were spreading, like some awful creeping infection! They were on both hands now. I shoved my hands deep into my coat pockets. I looked around – nobody was watching. So I started whistling casually, as if nothing had happened.

Then I caught sight of my reflection in the glass side of the tank.

'I don't believe this! I'm a freak! I'm an alien!'

Climbing up my neck, from under my T-shirt, was a wavy line of chocolate brown. Followed by white. Followed by –

'*Aaaargh!*' I zipped my coat right up. I put my hood up and pulled the drawstring tight so that there was only a tiny little hole to see out of.

I rushed up to Dad and grabbed his arm. 'Come on, Dad, come on! We've got to go!'

Dad looked down. 'I can't go now, George. I'm doing some research on this fish thing. Getting a few facts and figures.'

'Never mind that!' I gabbled at him through the hole in the hood. I rushed for the door.

Dad strode after me into the car park.

'Look, George,' he said. 'I'm trying to be reasonable here. Doing my best to understand. But what's going on? I thought you wanted fish for your birthday.'

'I *am* a fish,' I babbled at him from inside my coat.

'What?' Dad looked even more confused than ever. He looked out of his depth.

'Come on,' I said, tugging at the door handle. 'Open this car. I've got to get home. I've got to make an urgent phone call to Aunt Primrose.'

The car slid out of the car park of Pet World. I could see Dad staring at me in the driving mirror. He put on some classical music to calm himself down.

At home I raced up to the bathroom, locked the door and tore off my coat.

'Phew! Thank goodness!'

I breathed a big sigh of relief. The Neapolitan ice-cream stripes had gone. I checked in the bathroom mirror. I wasn't a freak. Or an alien. I was back to normal.

I touched my neck, where the stripes had been, just to make sure.

Then I snatched my hand back as if it were red hot.

My hand crept up to my neck again.

I turned sideways, looked in the mirror and lifted up the hair behind my ears ...

Then I went racing downstairs again.

'Mum! Mum!'

Mum wasn't in the kitchen. But Dad was. He was opening and shutting doors, looking for something.

I tugged at his shirt. 'Dad, Dad, what happened when you were eleven? Did anything weird happen to you? Did you get webbed toes, or fins or anything? Did you get slime glands?'

'Do you know where Mrs Perkins keeps the coffee?' asked Dad, with his head stuck in a cupboard.

I rushed into the living-room.

Mum was on the telephone. 'Shhhhh,' she warned. 'This is work.'

I jiggled about. I couldn't help myself. I had to grab my right hand to stop it feeling about behind my ear.

At last, Mum put down the phone.

'I've got lumps behind my ear!' I yelled at her. 'Behind both my ears!'

'All right, George. No need to deafen me. Just calm down.'

Mum felt my neck. '*Hmmm*,' she said. She felt my forehead.

'What are they?' I begged her. 'What do you think they are?'

Mum shrugged. 'Swollen glands,' she suggested. 'Have you got a cold or something?'

I forced myself to cough. '*Harumph! Harumph!* Yes, I think I have!'

I felt weak with relief. I'd just got a cold, that was

all. Just an ordinary boring old cold. Everybody gets *them*.

'Well, I hope you don't have to stay off school,' said Mum. 'It would be very inconvenient right now. You're not faking it, are you?'

'Of course I'm not! How can I fake lumps?'

'Well, I've got to admit you're a very peculiar colour,' said Mum. 'Do you feel ill or anything? Could it be all those crabsticks you've been eating?'

'What colour?' I gasped in a sort of strangled voice. 'What colour am I?'

I tried very hard to feel ill. But I didn't feel ill at all. I felt horribly healthy.

'You're a sort of green,' said Mum. 'Lime green in fact. And wait a minute, you're a sort of yellow as well. Bright yellow! It's quite spectacular! I've never seen anything like it!'

'I've got to make a phone call,' I said, weakly. 'A private one, in the study.'

And I staggered on bendy legs through the study door.

# Chapter Fourteen

With trembling fingers I punched in Aunt Primrose's number.

The phone rang and rang.

'Please be there,' I wished. 'Please be there.'

Then she picked up the phone. 'Hello?'

Her voice was as clear as the bathing pool. She could have been standing right next to me.

'Aunt Primrose, Aunt Primrose, I've got to talk to you. Strange things are happening to me. Uncontrollable things. I've got this book called *Growing Up*. It says about getting hairy and getting a deeper voice. But it doesn't say anything about green and yellow stripes and–'

'Ah, George,' interrupted Aunt Primrose calmly. 'Happy eleventh birthday, George. I was expecting you to call.'

'I'm a freak!' I gabbled into the phone. 'I keep changing colour!'

'Congratulations,' said Aunt Primrose in the same calm voice. 'And you are definitely NOT a freak. You are special. I told you that.'

'But I don't want to be special! I don't want to be different at all! People that are different get picked on. I mean, what will they think at school? You even get picked on for wearing specs. What's it going to be like if I get slime glands or something? They'll think I'm an alien from the planet Zarg!'

'For heaven's sake,' said Aunt Primrose. 'You must get things in perspective. We all have our little differences. Some people have belly-buttons that go in. Some people have belly-buttons that stick out. But they're not freaks, are they?'

'I'm not talking about belly-buttons!' I roared down the phone. 'I'm talking about—' Then a truly terrible thought burst into my brain. 'I won't turn into a Sea Hag, will I? I won't get tentacles, will I?'

'Absolutely not!' said Aunt Primrose, firmly. 'Whatever gave you that idea? Poor Violet was a one-off. She was quite exceptional.'

'What will I get then?'

'Oh,' said Aunt Primrose, 'just the usual things that run in the family. Nothing out of the ordinary. The changing colour thing. And perhaps gills, if you're lucky. Have you got any suspicious lumps?'

'Yes,' I said. 'But they're swollen glands. Mum said so.'

'I wouldn't bet on it,' said Aunt Primrose.

'But I've got a cold!' I coughed down the phone. '*Harumph! Harumph!*'

'We'll see,' said Aunt Primrose.

'But I'll be a freak! How can I be anything else? With gills and wavy lines all over me like a telly that's gone wrong. People will point at me in the street. They'll laugh at me. They'll say, "There goes George, that Fishy Freak!"'

'No, they won't,' insisted Aunt Primrose. 'They won't even notice. The colour changes are a bit alarming at first. But you can control them. I'll teach you how. And no one need see your gills. Just keep your hair long, that's all. And another tip. Don't practise jet propulsion in the bath. You can have a very nasty accident that way.'

'Jet propulsion? Will I be able to do that?'

'You might.'

'Wow!' I said. I couldn't help thinking how impressed my friends would be, when I jet-propelled in the swimming pool.

'And you might even get bio-luminescence,' added Aunt Primrose cheerily.

'What's that?' I asked suspiciously.

'Lots of deep-sea fishes have it. It means that bits of your body glow in the dark.'

'Which bits?'

'Well, I'm not sure. You'll have to wait to find out. That way, it'll be a big surprise, won't it?'

'Yes,' I said, in a stunned voice. 'A very big surprise ...'

'See?' interrupted Aunt Primrose. 'You're beginning to look on the bright side now, aren't you? To see the advantages. You can scuba-dive without the scuba! Just don't do it in the swimming baths, that's all. The lifeguard will think you're drowning. Save it for when you come here, to Two Sisters Cove.'

'I'm coming in two weeks,' I told her. 'I can stay for nearly all summer.'

'Perfect,' said Aunt Primrose. 'We've got a lot of talking to do.'

'Shall I tell Mum and Dad?' I asked her. 'You know, about being special?'

'I wouldn't bother,' said Aunt Primrose. 'They'll only think it's inconvenient.'

'OK,' I said, relieved.

'And whatever you do, don't worry! It's not so bad, having cuttlefish skills. It's very good fun actually.'

'Another thing,' I said. 'Another thing I want to ask you. Why isn't Dad a cuttlefish?'

'Oh, he's just unlucky,' said Aunt Primrose. 'He didn't inherit the family talents. They skip some people. Don't know why. He's an accountant, isn't he?'

'Yes.'

'Ah, well,' said Aunt Primrose mysteriously. 'That probably explains it then.'

# Chapter Fifteen

Aunt Primrose and I were taking an early morning stroll round Two Sisters Cove.

I'd been there for two days. And in that time I'd done nothing but ask questions, questions and more questions.

I asked her another one. 'What happened to the Sea Hag's precious?'

Aunt Primrose knew exactly what I meant.

'Oh, I let her octopus go,' she said. 'I let everything in the cellar go – the puffer fish and the electric eel and the cobra shark. She only kept them for company – for someone to talk to. And for when she got peckish, of course.'

I shivered. Sometimes I felt really sorry for the Sea Hag. And other times, I knew that what Aunt Primrose said was true. You couldn't trust her an inch.

I said, for about the millionth time, 'I'm glad I won't become a Sea Hag.'

'You might not even become a cuttlefish,' said Aunt Primrose. 'Those lumps behind your ear don't seem to be doing much. Perhaps your mum was right. Perhaps they are just swollen glands after all.'

I felt one of the lumps. I was sure I could feel four little ridges. I would be sorry if they didn't turn into gills. I'd got used to the idea of being different. I was even looking forward to it. I couldn't wait to see my friends' faces when I jet-propelled in swimming lessons. Or when bits of my body glowed in the dark.

'Will I get slime glands?' I asked Aunt Primrose hopefully.

She had told me that some eels have slime glands. And they can fill a bucket with green slime in two minutes!

But Aunt Primrose shook her head. 'Very, very unlikely,' she said.

'At least I can do the colour changes,' I said proudly.

I frowned. I was concentrating hard. Starting from my fingertips I made a wave of bright blue go galloping up my arm. Followed by a wave of green and a wave of raspberry pink. Then as a grand finale I made my face break out in jumping purple spots.

'Bravo!' smiled Aunt Primrose. 'You've been practising. Soon I'll teach you how to talk to fishes. But don't go chatting to any cobra sharks.'

'No way!' I said. 'Not unless I take my specs off first.'

We walked a bit further along the beach.

Then I said, 'I've got another question, I'm afraid.'

'Fire away,' said Aunt Primrose.

'Do you remember when I was little you came to our house?'

'Yes, I remember.'

'And you asked me a riddle – *The more you take, the more you leave behind*?'

'Yes.'

'Well, what's the answer to that riddle?'

'Look behind you, George,' she said.

I turned round. All I could see was a wide empty beach with two lines of footprints on it. I was puzzled for a minute.

Then I gave a big grin. I said, 'I know! I know the answer! The answer is footprints, isn't it? Footprints in the sand.'

'That's right,' said Aunt Primrose.

'That's easy-peasy!' I said. 'Why didn't I guess that before? It was so simple. And I was trying to make it difficult.'

'Some things are like that,' said Aunt Primrose. 'You worry away, making things difficult, making them ever so complicated. When really, it's all very simple.'

I knew what she was talking about. 'You mean, like colour-changing? Like having gills and stuff?'

'That's right,' she said. 'There's nothing to it.'

'Nothing to it at all,' I agreed.

And we walked back to the house, talking all the way. While around us the sun turned Two Sisters Cove to gold.

Choosing a brilliant book
can be a tricky business...
but not any more

# www.puffin.co.uk

**The best selection of books at your fingertips**

## So get clicking!

Searching the site is easy – you'll find
what you're looking for at the click of a mouse,
from great authors to brilliant books and more!

# Read more in Puffin

For complete information about books available from Puffin – and Penguin – and how to order them, contact us at the appropriate address below. Please note that for copyright reasons the selection of books varies from country to country.

# www.puffin.co.uk

In the United Kingdom: Please write to Dept EP, Penguin Books Ltd,
Bath Road, Harmondsworth, West Drayton, Middlesex UB7 ODA

In the United States: Please write to Penguin Putnam Inc., P.O. Box 12289,
Dept B, Newark, New Jersey 07101–5289 or call 1–800–788–6262

In Canada: Please write to Penguin Books Canada Ltd,
10 Alcorn Avenue, Suite 300, Toronto, Ontario M4V 3B2

In Australia: Please write to Penguin Books Australia Ltd,
P.O. Box 257, Ringwood, Victoria 3134

In New Zealand: Please write to Penguin Books (NZ) Ltd,
Private Bag 102902, North Shore Mail Centre, Auckland 10

In India: Please write to Penguin Books India Pvt Ltd,
11 Panscheel Shopping Centre, Panscheel Park, New Delhi 110 017

In the Netherlands: Please write to Penguin Books Netherlands bv,
Postbus 3507, NL–1001 AH Amsterdam

In Germany: Please write to Penguin Books Deutschland GmbH,
Metzlerstrasse 26, 60594 Frankfurt am Main

In Spain: Please write to Penguin Books S. A., Bravo Murillo 19,
1° B, 28015 Madrid

In Italy: Please write to Penguin Italia s.r.l.,
Via Felice Casati 20, I–20124 Milano

In France: Please write to Penguin France S. A.,
17 rue Lejeune, F–31000 Toulouse

In Japan: Please write to Penguin Books Japan, Ishikiribashi Building,
2–5–4, Suido, Bunkyo-ku, Tokyo 112

In South Africa: Please write to Longman Penguin Southern Africa (Pty) Ltd,
Private Bag X08, Bertsham 2013